Fantasies Of My Best Friend's Dad: An Enemies to Lovers Romance

Lavender Skye

Table of Contents

Chapter One - Emmy

"Where the hell are you?" I mutter to myself, as I double-check the time. I don't know how much longer Lyla is going to make us wait, but if we don't get going soon, we're not going to make it to the cabin in time.

I can feel a few eyes on me as I stand in the airport, and I don't meet them. I'm sure she's going to be here any moment. She said she was going to meet us at the airport, but there's no sign of her.

"Have you heard from her?" Nathan asks me, and I shake my head, frowning.

"I have no idea where she is," I admit.

"Typical," Nathan sighs. "I don't know what I expected. I suppose I should know better than to rely on my daughter to turn up on time."

I chew my lip. His angry-dad thing is a little scary, even though I know I'm not the one it's aimed at. I silently send out a prayer to Lyla, telling her to get here already; she's meant to be arriving in Tuscany after finishing up her research project in Paris, but it looks like she's going to keep us waiting just a little longer. The flight she was meant to be on has already arrived, and there's still no sign of her.

"She'll have to make her own way up," Nathan remarks, shaking his head. "She needs to learn. She can't make us wait for her."

"Just a little longer," I plead with him. I don't know Nathan particularly well, beyond meeting him at a couple of Lyla's birthday parties, but he makes me nervous. He's worked as a banker for his entire adult life, according to Lyla, and he's learned not to take crap from anyone. Including his own daughter, it seems.

He looks at his watch again, and shakes his head, beginning to pace. I glance down at my phone once more, and, finally, I see Lyla calling.

"Thank God," I mutter, and I answer at once, hoping she's got a decent excuse for where the hell she is right now.

"Where are you?" I demand, before she can so much as get a word out.

"Emmy, I'm so sorry," she tells me. It sounds like she's in a bar or something, raising her voice to make sure it can be heard over the hubbub around her.

"I'm not going to make it to Tuscany."

"What?" I gasp. We've been planning this trip for months now, our first vacation after we finish with our studies. I've been looking forward to it for basically the entire last semester of college – a chance to get out of America and have a little fun with my best friend to blow off some steam now that we're finished with college.

"I've...met someone," she tells me, her voice beaming with delight. Even though I can't see her right now, I know she is smiling. I groan.

"Are you kidding me?" I ask. Lyla has a habit of falling for guys, throwing herself full force into relationships with them, and then getting her heart broken. I thought she might have known better by now, but clearly, that's wishful thinking.

"I know, I know, but this time it's real," she assures me. "I can't wait for you to meet him – his name is Pierre, she exclaims "you're going to love him..."

"So, you're not going to come to Tuscany?" I asked her, bluntly. I can feel my heart sinking. I should have known something like this was going to happen, should have guessed she had this in her, but I had thought, given how much we had agreed on and how much we had planned together, she would see this through. The cabin belongs to *her* father, after all, it's not like I can go up there myself.

"Not this time," she replies, sounding genuinely apologetic. "I have to stay here to see how things go with Pierre. But you can still use the cabin! Have a couple of weeks to yourself, decompress – you'll have loads of fun."

I peer over at her father, who hasn't noticed I'm on the phone. I'm sure if he knew what we were talking about, he would go crazy.

"And what am I supposed to tell your father?" I demand.

"Oh, don't let him know about Pierre," she replies quickly. "He gets so protective about me seeing anyone, I don't want him causing trouble. Just...make something up, okay?"

"Okay," I sigh, resigned. I'm here now, and it's not like I can just book a flight back to the US. I don't have the same money Lyla does, and I can't change my plans at the last second the way she can.

"Thank you, babe," she tells me. "I have to go, but – I'll fill you in on everything as soon as I see you, alright?"

"Alright," I reply, hollowly. I'm happy for her, I really am, if she's actually found someone who makes her happy the way she claims this guy does. But, after so many nights tending to her after another heartbreak, it's hard not to think it's going to end badly.

"I'm sorry," She blurts out. "I'll make it up to you as soon as we get together, okay? Drinks are on me. Speak to you soon!"

And with that, she hangs up. I glance over to find Nathan looking at me expectantly, and I know I'm going to have to come up with something quick.

"Uh, Lyla's still in Paris," I explain to him. That part is true, at least. "She's stuck there finishing up the project she was working on for her environmental science course."

His eyebrows shoot up, and I can tell he doesn't buy it. He knows his daughter, he knows what she's like, and he knows damn well I'm probably making all of this up to cover for her.

"So, she's not going to be here?" He asks, and I nod, wincing. I hate being the one who has to deliver this news to him. I don't want to lie to Nathan, he seems like the kind of guy who can see right through anything you try to spin to him to the truth.

His shoulders sag, and he shakes his head.

"I don't know what I expected with her," he mutters. I almost want to agree. I love Lyla, but if there's one thing I know for sure about her, she's a total flake.

"If you don't want me to stay at the cabin, that's fine," I tell him quickly. "I know it's for your family.

No, Lyla made a commitment," he replies, shaking his head. "The least I can do is see you through the parts of it I can."

I shift from foot to foot. I almost want to tell him I'd prefer it if he puts me on a flight back to America right now instead. I find him so seriously intimidating, and I'd be lying if I said the thought of spending a car trip all the way up to the Duffy family cabin exactly appeals to me. I doubt he's going to be in the best mood, either, given his daughter just flaked, and I am sure he has better things to do than run me around like a chauffeur.

But I don't have it in me to argue with him, not right now, anyway. And I didn't come all this way just to turn around and go home at the first turn. I've been looking forward to this trip for forever, and, after I worked my butt off for my degree, don't I deserve a little luxury to indulge myself on the other side?

"Sure," I agree, my voice a little higher than normal. I'm certain he can tell how nervous I am, and I hope I can conceal the obviousness of my anxiety now we're going to be spending some more time together.

He reaches for my bags, taking them from me without so much as a question. I smile. Okay, so at least he's a gentleman. I guess someone like him doesn't get as far as he has without learning some good old-fashioned manners.

"Come on," he tells me, jerking his head towards the car outside. "Let's get out of here."

Chapter Two – Nathan

I squint out of the front of the car, as the snow
starts to pile up on the window. The weather is
turning quickly, and I don't know how much
more of this I can take before I have to admit
defeat and turn back around.

"Is it usually this bad?" Emmy asks from beside
me, looking nervous. She's been mostly silent the
entire journey – she asked to put on the radio,
but I shot it down quickly, not wanting to deal
with the mindless thrumming of whatever music
happened to be in the top forty these days.

"Not usually," I mutter, as I carefully press down
on the accelerator to get us over the small bump.
Normally, the road is immaculately-maintained,
the snow brushed to the side to make way for
anyone coming through, but here, now, it doesn't
look like it normally does.

I suppose it is the season for it. It's coming up on
Christmas, and plenty of families retire to their
ski cabins in Tuscany to enjoy the weather and
get in the festive spirit. I thought I would just be
able to hand off Lyla and whatever friends she
had brought with her and get back to work, but
instead, I'm stuck in a car with a woman twenty

years my junior who doesn't seem to have a clue what to say to me.

Not that I am much better off right now, if I am being honest. It's not often I find myself with women her age. The line of work I've been in my whole life, most of the people in it are in their forties and fifties and older, focused on making their money and supporting their families as best they can.

"So, what is it you study?" I had asked her earlier in the drive, when I had still decided to try and make a little conversation.

"Uh, Art History," She replies. I held back a snort of amusement. It sounds like the most useless degree in the world for anything other than working at an art museum, and I wonder what she intends to do with it.

"That must have been interesting," I offered her, hoping she can't tell what's really going on in my head.

"You can say it sounds stupid," she told me bluntly. "Everyone else does."

I cocked an eyebrow. Sounds like she had to deal with a lot of derision in her line of study already. Maybe I could stand to be a little more understanding about it.

"No, it's...interesting," I replied, hoping I was selling my statement. I've spent long enough in business meetings with people who have no clue what they're talking about to have perfected faking my interest in something, even if I don't really care about it.

She glanced over at me, clearly not buying it.

"You're a banker, right?" She asked me, and I nodded.

"Yes, have been for the last twenty years."

"So I guess you don't have a lot of time for Art History," she remarked. She had seen right through me. I flashed her a brief smile.

"Guess you got me there."

We continued the drive to the cabin, which was a couple of hours away from the airport. I'm not sure what she's going to do when she gets up there – it's been so long since I was in college, it's hard to remember what I would have wanted right after I had graduated. Beer, probably? I have no idea if she's a big drinker, but I know my daughter is, and I'm sure if the two of them are as close as she claims, they were planning on putting away some serious booze while they're away.

I'm still not sure I believe the story Emily spun to me about where Lyla is. Finishing up her project? It just doesn't quite make sense to me. Sounds like the kind of thing someone might tell their friend's father to cover for something Lyla doesn't want me to know.

But, if I know one thing about Lyla, it's that trying to get the truth out of her when she doesn't want to hand it over is never going to get me far. It's been the same since she was a teenager, she's never been willing to tell me the little details of what's going on in her life, and maybe that's for the best. I'm sure if I knew the ins and outs of everything, I wouldn't be happy with how she was spending her would-be-study time.

I slow the car down as I make the final turn up to the cabin at the top of the Tuscany Hills. Ours is a decent distance from everyone else, so that when we come up here, it feels as though we're really getting a break from the rest of the world. I spend enough of my time stuck around people for business purposes, to know when I get away from them, I *really* want to be away from them.

"Is that it?" Emmy asks, as she squints through the flurries of snow falling around the car. I'm not going to be able to stay long, or else I'll get stuck up here.

"Yes, that's it," I tell her. "Come on, quickly – let's get inside and I can show you where everything is."

I'm still annoyed Lyla isn't here to do it for me, but at least I can make sure Emmy knows how to take care of this place while she's staying here. It's a small log cabin, with a path that leads right up on to the skiing slopes. Not that I imagine she'll be doing a lot of that, not in this weather.

She hooks her bags over her shoulder and follows me inside, lifting her hand to blow the snow from her face. She's shivering like crazy already, not dressed for the weather, and I wonder if Lyla gave her any kind of warning about how cold it could get up here. People heard Italy, and then just assumed it was all beachy sunshine and bright skies. At this time of year, though, it was anything but.

I press the code into the door to unlock it, and hustle her inside before she can catch a chill. Inside, she lets out a sigh of relief and dumps her bags at her feet, looking around to take the place in.

"Woah," she murmurs, as she gazes this way and that. "This place is…it's amazing."

I forget sometimes that not everyone has access to spots like this; I didn't grow up with access to this sort of luxury, but it's been so long since I've had it I've almost forgotten what it was like.

I glance outside, at the flurries of snow starting to build up around the windows. I'm not sure how I feel about driving back down to the airport in this, even though I know I needed to get back to work sooner rather than later. It just doesn't look entirely safe, and I'm not sure I want to risk putting myself in danger heading back down the mountain.

As she makes her way around the cabin, I pull out my phone to check to see if there's anything noted by the local authorities about when and where to drive – I can stay for a night, if I need to, take off first thing in the morning before she's awake. I don't want to stay any longer than I have to; passing the time with a recent college graduate isn't exactly my idea of a good time. But if I have to stick around a little longer, I can manage it...

I curse to myself when I see the messages posted on the local authority board. Shit – they're telling us not to drive at all if we can avoid it until the incoming blizzard has passed and they can get in to clear the roads. It doesn't say how long it's going to be before it lifts.

"What is it?" Emmy asks, her bright blue eyes widening with concern when she hears me muttering. Maybe she thinks I've busted Lyla.

"I'm going to have to stay here tonight," I told her. No need to admit it might be more than that, I'm sure she's already annoyed enough she has to put up with me for an evening, let alone anything more than that.

"Oh," she blurts out, clearly surprised. "I – is it the weather? Is it not safe?"

"Not right now," I reply. "I'm sure they'll get it all cleared by tomorrow morning, they usually take care of this stuff quickly."

"That's fine," she replies, offering me a smile. She has a nice smile. I can't help but notice it – it seems genuine, something I don't encounter a whole lot in my line of work. I appreciate that.

"So, which room do you want?" She asks as she gestures towards the two bedrooms. "You own the place. You get the first pick."

"How generous of you," I reply, trying to joke a little. She seems perfectly pleasant, and if I'm going to be stuck here for the foreseeable future, then I'm going to need to find some way to get along with her. She might not be the kind of person I chose to spend my time with, but I could manage this for a night or two.

Right?

Chapter Three – Emmy

I peer around the door, not sure what I'm expecting to see.

This trip has already gone completely against what I thought it would be. I had imagined some fun, chill, wine-soaked girls' vacation with Lyla, and instead, I'm snowed into her family's luxury cabin with her slightly-scary Dad.

I mean, at least the place is amazing. I know Lyla comes from a rich family, but sometimes, something like this comes along to remind me of it. The cabin, though it's not huge, looks as though it could have come right out of some interior design magazine, the polished dark wood and gold elements giving it this deliciously cozy feel. A large fireplace is surrounded by some giant armchairs, all of them equipped with their own giant, hand-knitted blanket. Even though I wish I could get out into the snow a little without freezing my butt off, this is a pretty good place to keep warm.

I've been tossing and turning all night, my mind racing as I try to work out the best way to deal with all of this. I get the feeling Nathan sees through everything I told him about what Lyla is up to, and I can't help but feel a little guilty lying to him. He's letting me stay in this beautiful place, after all, and I'm spinning stories to him about what his daughter is up to. Not exactly the best etiquette.

And now, I'm staying here with him. He's just a room away. It's not like we know each other well, and I'm nervous about what it's going to be like to spend more time with him. It doesn't seem like we have a whole hell of a lot in common, and I don't want to make a fool of myself in front of someone as established and respected as him. It's not like we're going to run into each other in the course of my career, but still – he's the kind of guy you want to keep on your side, no matter what.

The bedroom I'm staying in looks out onto the gorgeous, snow-dipped hills beyond the cabin, and waking up opposite them, it's hard to believe I'm really here. My stomach grumbles dangerously, and I decide to get up and forage for some food.

I feel like I'm at a sleepover as a kid, trying to work out when I can go downstairs and ask for breakfast. Knowing Lyla's Dad is here isn't making me feel any more mature. I peep around the door – and I find myself frozen to the spot when I see what is waiting for me on the other side.

It's him! Nathan. He's already up. And, by the looks of it, he's been up for long enough to get a good sweat going.

He's doing some cardio, stripped to the waist in nothing but a pair of sweatpants, and my God, he's in seriously good shape. I've only ever seen him in the smart suits and button-downs he usually wears, and catching a glimpse of him like this feels like peeping behind a curtain I'm not meant to be able to see behind. His strong chest is glistening with sweat, his arms flexing as he pushes himself back to his feet, and I swear I can see a whisper of abs on his stomach, too. I bit my lip. I know I shouldn't be staring like this, but, I mean, *look* at him...

With his cropped dark hair, strong jaw, and a smattering of salt-and-pepper stubble, he's the very definition of a hot dad. I've done my best not to notice it up until now, given that he's the father to my best friend, but with her nowhere to be seen and him dripping sweat right in front of me, it only seems right I enjoy the sight of him a little.

It's been a long, long time since I've actually been with a guy, and I guess my thirstiness is showing a little. I've been so focused on my studies, I just haven't had time to think about dating or anything, and being presented with a good-looking dude right in front of me...yeah, that's not exactly what I was expecting.

I push open the door and clear my throat, letting him know I'm there. I don't want him to think I've been spying on him or anything, even if I might have snuck more of a look than I should have. He reaches for a towel beside him and presses it against his bare chest, not bothering to cover up.

"Oh, Emily, you're awake," he replies, catching his breath.

"You can call me Emmy," I tell him. Now I've seen him half-naked, it only feels right we cut to the chase a little.

"Did you sleep well?" He asks me, finally reaching for a shirt.

"Yeah, I slept okay," I lied quickly. No need for him to know the truth of everything running through my head right now. I can keep all of that to myself.

"Is there something I could have for breakfast?" I ask. "I'm starving."

"Do you think I'd have let my daughter stay here without making sure she had food?" He asks, raising his eyebrows at me.

"No, I was just wondering," I reply, feeling a little embarrassed. I don't want him to think I'm judging him or his family. I just need something to eat.

"Yes, there's food in the kitchen," he replies. "Take what you want."

He heads to the bathroom to get himself cleaned up, and I stick my tongue out at him behind his back. Yeah, I remember now why I find him so intimidating. There's something sharp about him, spiky around the edges, as though he wants everyone to know how in charge he is of everything in his life.

I make my way to the kitchen and make myself some eggs and bacon, as well as brew a giant pot of coffee; I feel like I'm going to need it if I'm going to get through the rest of the day without passing out on my feet. I hum to myself as I cook, filling the kitchen with the scent of food, and starting to relax a little. Even if Lyla's not here, I can still have a good time, right?

This is about blowing off steam after spending the last few months of my life dedicated to making sure I actually got my degree. Now it's in the bag, and I officially have my BA, I'm going to relax a little. My parents offered to have me come stay with them for a bit while I got on my feet, and I might take them up on it after all of this is over, but the thought of moving back into my childhood home right now, when I was supposed to be starting my adult life just didn't feel right.

Besides, their whole house is about the size of this cabin, and I know we'd be on top of each other the entire time. It seems like Nathan wants to put as much space between the two of us as possible, and I am more than happy to oblige.

He emerges from the shower a little after I have sat down to eat, and I gesture to the coffee sitting on the counter.

"There's a fresh pot for you, if you want some," I tell him, and he shakes his head.

"I quit coffee years ago," he replies, a little dismissive. "I don't need to rely on that stuff to get me out of bed in the morning."

"Well, some of us do," I joke, lifting my cup playfully. He doesn't respond, heading over to the fridge to make himself some breakfast. I sigh to myself. How long is he going to be kicking around here, again? I'm not sure I can take much more of his attitude, and I'm sure he wants rid of me sooner rather than later.

He heads into the bedroom again to make some calls, and I decide to arrange my stuff so I can take a long bath with one of the books I packed for the trip – I really want to make this as relaxing as possible, it just looks like I'm going to have to avoid him to do it.

Outside, the snow is piling up, and I wonder how he's going to get back down the mountain in this weather. I almost want to ask him, but I get the feeling he doesn't want to be reminded of how he's stuck here with me. He doesn't seem like the type who would much appreciate it.

He's probably obsessed with his work. I know he's got some serious money to his name, probably in the billions, and I don't even want to think how much time and effort it must take to maintain it. No wonder he's not married – after

Lyla's mother split with him, he probably hasn't had the time to see anyone else.

Which is a damn shame. I'm sure there are plenty of women out there who would kill to just go for dinner with someone like him. He's rich, he's hot, he's got a good job, and his daughter is long since out of the house. I mean, he's perfect.

For someone. Not for me, obviously.

I run myself a bath, dripping in a generous amount of the bath oil I brought with me and sinking beneath the warm water with my book. I close my eyes, tip my head back, and let out a long sigh. See? This is what I came here for. I can just kick back, and forget about everything else for a while.

I know It's not going to be easy for me to find work when I get back into the real world, but I'm trying not to think about it. I have put in a few applications at local galleries, hoping I can find a way to turn my degree into a real job, but it's not likely. Art History is a passion for me, and I've long since concluded that it's not going to be easy – or even possible – for me to turn it into long-term work. I don't mind working retail or something if I have to, but I hope I can find a way to make it something more permanent...

Not that I'm thinking about that right now, not a chance in hell, because I am here to chill out and relax and kick back. I turn on some music and flick through my book, quietly singing along and hoping I'm not annoying Nathan too much.

If I'm being honest with myself, this morning isn't the first time I've noticed how handsome he is. Of course, I've done everything I can to push down my attraction to him, because he's Lyla's dad and I'm not going to be the creep who starts hitting on the parents of the people they're friends with, but still – there's something about him I like. Something about those sharp gray eyes and his strong hands that makes it hard for me to think of anything else.

As I lay back in the bath, I find my mind drifting toward the sight of his body. His strength, his power. I can almost imagine how it might feel to run my hand over his stomach, feel the muscles beneath his skin. Before I know it, my hand is sliding down over my belly and between my legs, even though I know this is wrong, even though I should know better...

Suddenly, a loud knock on the door pulls me out of my reverie, and I blink and sit up straight.

"What is it!" I yell, feeling a bit annoyed.

"Can you turn down that music?" He says. "I'm trying to take a work call right now."

"Yes, sure, sorry," I snap back. I can feel the flush spreading over my cheeks, as though somehow he's going to know what I've been getting up to in here.

Good thing he stopped me. No way is it a good idea for me to start getting off to the thought of him. I need to get through the next day or so, and he's going to be out of here. Nothing more to it than that.

That evening, and the snow has piled up even more against the doors; I can't see any way that he's going to be able to get out anytime soon, and he seems to be of the same mind. He casts a look towards the car, still parked outside, which is practically buried under a foot or two of snow.

"You want to make some dinner?" "I ask?" While, trying to keep my voice bright. I know he's annoyed right now, and I get it, I do. He's pissed that he's stuck here with me. But the least we can do is try to get along.

"I'm not hungry," he replies, a little sharply. I roll my eyes at him.

"You haven't had anything since breakfast," I point out. "You need to eat. Come on, let me make you something. You can help, if you want."

He seems a little taken aback by how blunt I am about this, but I'm not going to let him mope the whole time he's here. If we're going to be staying here together, I am going to find a way for the two of us to get along.

I start putting together a simple pasta dish, and, to my surprise, he comes over to help chop some of the vegetables. I'm a little surprised he even knows how to cook; I'd imagine he'd have staff to take care of all these kinds of things for him back home.

We serve up a quick meal, and sit down at the table together – it's small enough that our knees are almost touching beneath it, and I can't help but notice how much it feels like a date. Does he see it, too? I hope not.

"Thanks for this," he mutters, as he gestures to the food in front of us. "I have a hard time eating sometimes when I'm stressed."

"You're stressed?" I ask.

"Of course I am," he replies. "I'm stuck here, away from work, and it looks like the storm is going to set in even worse tomorrow. It could be days before we get out of here. Weeks, even."

My heart twists in my chest. I know it's not a good thing, but I actually don't mind the thought of sticking it out here a little longer with him. Maybe it's just the freedom I've got from my studies, or maybe it's something else entirely, but I'm enjoying myself.

"Weeks," I echo after him, shaking my head. "That's crazy. Do we have enough food to last us that long, if it comes to it?"

"I think so," he replies. "We might have to make a trek to one of the stores, but if we're careful, we should be able to make it work."

We. I like it when he talks about us like that. I'm not quite sure why, but there's something reassuring about it. Being stuck up here, in the middle of nowhere, in a country I have never been to before without the friend who was supposed to guide me through it, is more than a little scary, but at least I have him here to keep me company.

"We should," I agree, and I glance up at him. Do I dare tell him we need to actually try to get on for that to happen? I get the feeling he wouldn't take too kindly to being told what to do, but I don't want him to act as though I'm just some annoyance hanging off his arm the entire time.

He sighs heavily, and meets my gaze.

"I'm sorry about this," he tells me, finally. "I didn't expect my daughter to bail on you, and I'm sure the two of you had plenty more fun plans than...this."

"It's okay," I promise. "You couldn't know this was what was going to happen. Besides, this is a good chance for me to relax after college. Not like I can obsess over my grades when we're snowed in up here, right?"

He nods, slowly, and I think he's starting to see this for what it is. It doesn't have to be some nightmare. Yes, it's not exactly what either of us wanted, but we can make it work, if we stick together and navigate through it.

"I suppose you're right," he agrees. "Maybe this can be a break from work for me, too."

"Something tells me you don't take many of those," I remark, and he laughs. I haven't heard him laugh much, and I instantly take a liking to it. There's something warm and bright about his laugh, confident, and it seems to light up his whole being.

"Yeah, you're right," he agrees, as he takes a bite of his food. "This is delicious, by the way."

"Thank you," I reply, and I feel a little heat rising in my chest. I am sure I would do well to ignore it, but there is a part of me that wants to acknowledge this as the intimate moment it is – a part of me that wants him to notice how close we are right now, how easy it would be for our knees to be touching beneath the table if we just moved an inch.

But maybe it's better if we ignore it. Because I'm not sure what it would mean for him to notice that.

Or for him to spot how much my eyes are lingering on him across the table right now.

Chapter Four – Nathan

I wake up to the burning brightness of the fresh snow outside, and the sound of Emmy singing to herself in the kitchen. And, as I lay there in bed and listen, I can't help but smile a little.

This is…peaceful. Surprisingly so. I'm not normally the kind of guy who stays in bed for longer than a minute after he wakes up, ready to jump out of bed and get into my day, but there's not much for me to do as long as I'm here. Maybe it's better for me to just relax a little, take some time to chill out for a change.

Like she said, it's not as though I take a lot of time to do that, in my line of work. I don't have the space to relax, not with all the pressure on my shoulders. I'm still getting used to the strangeness of being out here, knowing there's nothing I can do but sit back and take a little time to myself for a change. I've been in touch with the office back home, and made it clear there's not much I can do as long as I'm up here. The storm will clear when it clears, and until then, I'm very much trapped.

Trapped with Emmy, of all people. I barely know her, not really, but I suppose I'm going to have to start now we're all but living together. My daughter's best friend – I suppose it would be a good idea for me to have a clue about who she's spending time with.

And Emmy seems...nice. Maybe a little thoughtless, given how loudly she was playing music before, but nice. She insisted on the two of us having dinner together the night before, and, with the amount of stress I'm under, I know I would have skipped it if it hadn't been for her, so I was grateful.

I'm not the best at taking care of myself. No, I've mostly been focused on looking after Lyla, and making sure the business is ticking over, and that doesn't leave a whole lot of time for anything else. Normally, it doesn't bother me, but sometimes, I feel the toll it's taking on my body, especially as I'm getting older.

Especially since the divorce.

I push the thought away quickly. I'm not going to let that get to me, I'm not going to think about it right now. Just like Emmy came out here to relax after her graduation, maybe this could be a chance for me to forget what I was leaving behind, too.

I climb out of bed and grab a tee and jeans, throwing them on before I head out to the kitchen. I pause for a moment before I greet her.

She's wearing a tank top and some sweatpants that look well lived-in, but there's something cute to me about how comfortable she is here.

Her soft, pale skin looks like it's been bathed in cream, and her hair is pulled back from her face, a few tendrils escaping to tease at the back of her neck. I can almost imagine brushing them away with my fingers, but I push the thought down swiftly.

"Morning," I greet her, and she turns around and smiles as she sees me emerging from my room.

"Hey!," She replies brightly. "Do you want something to eat? I'm making pancakes..."

I hesitate. It's been a hell of a long time since I had pancakes, and I can practically hear my trainer in my ear, telling me to focus on something with more balanced macros so I can work on my body comp goals.

But my trainer isn't here right now. No, the only person with me is Emmy, and if she wants me to have pancakes with her, then I am sure as hell going to have pancakes with her.

"That'd be great," I agree. "Thank you."

She serves me up a generous helping and hands me a bottle of maple syrup she managed to dig out of the cupboard – the two of us head over to the small dining table, and she crosses her legs, drawing my attention to her bare feet as they dangle over the edge of the chair.

"So, what's the news on the storm?" She asks me with interest.

"No updates as of yet," I reply. "Looks like it's going to keep coming down for the rest of the day."

She pulls a face.

"I was hoping I could call my mom and let her know I'm okay, but I don't have any phone signal in the cabin," she sighs. "Do you know if there's anywhere nearby I could get it?"

"I don't think you should be going out in this weather at all," I warn her. "You could freeze. Trust me, if you're not used to it, this kind of cold can hit you hard."

"Right," she replies, vaguely, but I can tell she doesn't quite believe me. I wish there was some way I could get it through to her, let her know I'm not just saying this, but I remember all too well what it's like to be young. To feel like you can take on anything in the world, and not have to worry about the consequences.

We have breakfast together, and she asks me a little about my work – she sounds genuinely interested, which surprises me. Most people glaze over when they find out I work in banking, but she listens with interest, peppering a few more questions in as we go.

"It sounds like it must take up all your time," she remarks, and I nod.

"Ever since Lyla left home, for sure."

Truth be told, I'm pretty sure that's what led to the divorce, though I'm sure Emmy doesn't want to hear about it. My now-ex, Natalie, started drifting away from me as soon as Lyla left home. I'm not surprised, because a part of me realized that the two of us were only really hanging on to each other for our daughter.

And now, with her at college and graduated, we just don't have that much in common anymore.

She found someone else. Of course she did. She's never been the kind of woman to sit around and wait for things to happen, she goes out there and gets them, and when she decided she wanted a new lover, she didn't wait for my approval. I came home from the office one day to find the two of them drinking wine together in our penthouse apartment, and Natalie told me it was over. She wanted a divorce.

That was last year, and I'm still reeling from it. I know she's moved on, but I have no idea how I'm supposed to do the same, if I even have it in me to move on the way she did. Do I have the time to find someone else? I feel like my life is so chaotic as it is, it would be wrong to go looking for someone who can put up with it. Better for me to keep my head down, focus on supporting Lyla, and making sure the business stays ticking over. Those are the things that matter to me.

I insist on doing the washing up after breakfast, and she leans on the counter beside me and watches as I clean up after her.

"You know, I could get used to this," she jokes lightly. "Someone tidying up my mess."

"You want to hire me?" I joke. "I do a pretty good job. And my rates are cheap."

"They'd have to be," she replies, as she points to a spot I left on the plate I was cleaning. "Given the state, this is in. You call yourself a dishwasher?"

I laugh. Emmy has a good sense of humor, and I appreciate it. I feel as though I've been all too serious these last couple of years, especially with the divorce, I've almost forgotten what it feels like to just let loose and have fun. Maybe, as long as I'm here, I can do just that, kick back and relax and leave everything else behind.

Emmy slips into a bath after breakfast, and I pull out my laptop to check my emails. I don't want to fall too behind on anything; if I can help it.

And there is something about knowing she is naked just a few feet away from me that's making it hard to think straight.

I mean, I'm still a red-blooded man. And I would be blind not to notice that she's gorgeous. I'm sure she wouldn't even look twice at a guy like me, a guy my age, but I can't pretend I don't see how striking she is.

No doubt she's got someone back home. No way a girl like her has been able to stay single, I'm sure she's got a line of suitors up and down the block, just waiting for her to return.

But for now, she's here with me, and there's something about that I like. An intimacy, in just spending this time with her, passing a few hours together, cooking and cleaning together. It's been a hell of a long time since I actually got to know someone new, and I have to admit, I like it. It helps that she's got a sense of humor and some smarts, for sure. I don't know a whole lot of people from her generation outside of my daughter, but most of the ones I have encountered tend to be a little more self-serious. I appreciate her brightness, and how she doesn't seem to put too much on her shoulders.

Plus, she's downright gorgeous. Nothing wrong with noticing that, right? Nothing wrong with being honest with myself about the way she looks. It's been a while since I've let myself be around a woman in anything other than a professional setting, and my instincts are kicking in just the way they always did. The soft curves of her body, the way her hair falls over her shoulders when she tosses her head back and laughs, the fullness of her bottom lip – it all makes it hard to think straight when she's around.

I keep my head down as she emerges from the bathroom, wrapped in nothing but a towel, but I can't help but steal a glance at her. Her skin is glistening with wetness, and I have to bite my lip to keep from saying something. Her legs, long and slim, look even more tempting, and I promise myself I am going to keep focused on my work.

Because if I let myself get distracted by her? I'm sure we're going to land in a mess even bigger than the snowstorm tearing things up outside this window.

Chapter Five – Emmy

I frown at my phone, wrinkling my nose as I try to work out how to get this thing to work.

I know my mom will be worried sick about me, especially since she hasn't heard from me since I left America. I promised her I would be in touch as often as I could, and I've got no doubt she's seen the snowstorm that pulled in over the cabin, and has managed to invent a million different possibilities about what has happened to me.

I don't want her worried. I need to talk to her, even just to fire off a text to let her know she's got nothing to worry about. But I have been around this cabin what feels like ten times, and I still haven't been able to find the spot I can get signal in.

I peer outside, into the snow, and chew my lip. I know Nathan said I shouldn't go out there, but how else am I going to get in touch with her, really? The last thing I want is for her to be freaking out, thinking something terrible has happened to me, when I'm actually in this luxury cabin, relaxing and feeling pretty damn great.

Just ten minutes outside, right? Not far. I don't have to go running over the whole mountain to find a signal, I just need a blip of it to send off a message, and then I'll be done. I know it's cold out there, but I'm sure I can handle it. I'll bundle myself up in a bunch of clothes, and take a nice warm bath when I get back.

I head to my bedroom to go grab as many cozy clothes as I can; and start slapping them on. I can hear Nathan next door, in the middle of a work call, and I curse that my mom still doesn't have internet, or else I'd just be able to shoot her an email and be done with this.

But for now, I'm relying on my phone, and I don't want to keep her waiting any longer than I already have. I glance at Nathan's door before I go, wondering if I should let him know where I'm headed, but I'm sure he'd just tell me to get right back inside before I froze to death out there. He's way too worried about it, I'm sure I'll be fine. It's just a little snow. I can handle snow.

I pull on an extra pair of socks and slip into my boots, and then step out of the front door. I gasp as soon as the wind hits my face, my skin aching with coldness at once. I stuffed my hands into my pocket and squinted against the near-blinding brightness of the snow, and started to walk.

Okay. Not far. Not far, and I would be able to get the signal I need. I can already feel the shivers starting deep in my system, and I try to ignore them. No need to panic. I don't need to turn this into something it's not. It's just a few minutes outside, I'm not some delicate little flower that'll wilt the first moment I step into the cold. I'm fine, see?

I tramp through the thick snow in my boots, but they do little to keep me dry – I can already feel the wetness in my jeans as the snow leaks through the denim and onto my skin. My teeth are starting to chatter, and I pull out my phone to check if I have a signal. Nothing yet. Shit. I need to go further...

I continue along my way, taking my time, holding the phone out in front of me and sweeping it around in the hopes of finding something that looks right. I don't need much, just a quick second of signal, and I think I can get this done.

I can feel the wind chill starting to set in around my bones, and the shivers begin in earnest. I can't stay out here much longer. I squint against the white of the snow, but it's all starting to look the same to me now. I glance over my shoulder, to see if my tracks lead back to the house, but I can hardly make them out underneath the snow falling around me.

A gust breezes in and digs beneath my clothes, and I wrap my jacket a little tighter around me. I can't be out here much longer, I don't want to be. Maybe Nathan was right, and I should have known better than to step outside the warmth of the cabin...

He doesn't even know where I am right now. A cold wash of panic hits me, as I stuff my phone back into my pocket, unable to see anything on it through the flurries of snow anyway. How far have I gone from the cabin? I don't even know, but I don't like this, not one little bit.

My jeans are sopping and stuck to me, the icy wetness making my whole body tremble. My vision s starting to blur as I made my way back toward the cabin. I'm going in the right direction, aren't I? I'm not even sure. Why didn't I look where I was going? I feel like I am going to lose it...

I trek through the snow, my boots filling with half-melted wetness, and I curse that I didn't tell Nathan where I was going. He would have stopped me, I was sure of it. Maybe I should have listened to him.

But it's too late for that now. All I can do is keep pushing forward, and find some way to make it back to the cabin. I'm sure it can't be too far away. How long have I been walking, anyway? I was so focused on getting a signal, I hardly noticed how long my feet had been moving beneath me.

I can feel my legs starting to get shaky, and panic grips me. Shit. What the hell am I going to do? I need to get out of here, I need to get back into the warmth and safety of the cabin, but I don't have a clue where I'm going. I look around, and it all seems the same to me, white as far as the eye can see.

Panic starts to take hold. I don't know how I am going to get back to the cabin. It all just feels impossible. The cold is gripping deep in my chest, and I can feel my heart starting to pick up the pace. Beneath my clothes, my skin is prickling almost painfully, and I want nothing more than to just be in a warm bath, stop all this, and forget I even stepped out of the front door.

"Emmy, Emmy you there!"

I hear a voice call my name, but I hardly have the strength to respond. How can the cold work this quickly? It doesn't feel as though it should be possible. I croak out a response, but I'm sure it's not enough for whoever is calling to me to hear me.

I sink to my knees in the snow, the cold rushing up and through my system as I try to stop it. I can't see straight, I can't speak, and my skin feels like it is about to peel away from the bone with the chill. The last thing I feel before I close my eyes is a pair of strong arms around me, and I sink into them gratefully, thanking God for whoever has found me.

Chapter Six – Nathan

I scoop her up into my arms, and hold her against my chest, squinting against the flurries of snow rushing around us. It's not far back to the cabin, but I don't want to waste a moment. She's clearly freezing, and I'm just relieved I could get to her in time.

As soon as I realized she wasn't in the cabin, I went out to find her. I know she can't handle this, I know she isn't equipped for the cold. She hasn't been somewhere like this before, and she doesn't know how brutal the elements can be, especially when the wind is as bad as this.

She's shaking against me as I stumble back to the cabin, but at least she's still moving. She's in a pair of jeans and a jacket, nothing like what she needs to brace for the cold out here, and it's no wonder the chill set in so quickly.

"You silly girl," I mutter to her, as I carry her back through the snow. She winds her arms around my neck, hanging on tight, and I can feel her warm breath against my neck, coming hard and fast.

As soon as we're back into the cabin, I close the door behind us and look around for a way to get her warmed up. The fire is almost out, and I don't want to spend the time to get it going – she needs to be brought back to temperature quickly, or else she's going to end up frostbitten.

The bath. A lukewarm bath, to ease her into the warmth again, that's what she needs right now. I gently lay her on the couch, covering her with a blanket for the time being, and hurry to the bathroom to start filling the tub.

I check the water is the right temperature – if I go too hot, she might get chilblains, and I don't want her in any more discomfort than she already is. I don't know what she was thinking, going out there into the cold when she must have known how dangerous it was, but I could remember all too well what it was like to be young like that, to feel as though you were invincible. Maybe she thought it wouldn't affect her. Well, now, she knew different. I hope she would listen to me next time.

As I get the bath running, I go back out to check on her. She is trembling violently on the couch, and I lay a hand gently on her shoulder, letting her know I'm there.

"I'm getting a bath ready for you," I tell her softly. "You need some help getting into it?"

She nods, still not quite able to get the words out. I reach down to help her up, and she slumps against me, her body a block of ice.

I take her through to the bathroom, and she sheds her jacket and then peels off her top – I avert my eyes, not wanting her to feel like I'm just trying to get a look at her body when she's clearly struggling.

She lets out a sigh of annoyance, and I glance over to see her fumbling with the button of her jeans – her fingers are so cold they are clumsy, and she can't get them undone.

"Here, let me," I tell her, and I reach out to undo them. My fingers skim briefly over a strip of her frigid skin, the spot just above her pants, and I try not to think about how naked she is right now, how exposed she is to me.

I need to keep it together. This isn't about me or my attraction to her, this is about making sure she doesn't get too cold. It's important we get the chill out of her system before it sets in, or she could be in real trouble. She needs my help right now, not for me to look at her with lust in my eyes.

She pushes off her jeans and then the soaked panties underneath, and quickly pulls off her bra before she slides into the water. Her teeth are chattering as she climbs in, wrapping her arms around her knees and pulling them into her chest. She looks miserable, her hair plastered to her face as she starts to come back to the real world. I almost want to scold her, but she's a grown adult, and she doesn't need me telling her off right now. She knows she made a mistake, and she doesn't have to hear it from anyone else.

I sit on the edge of the tub to keep an eye on her as she warms up, making sure not to let my eyes linger too long on any part of her naked body. I'm not doing this just to get her naked, I'm doing this to keep her well. The last thing we need, being stuck up here, is for her to catch a chill and need medical treatment. I'm just doing what I can to try and avoid that happening.

Slowly, her teeth start to slow down, and the trembling begins to subside a little. She's beginning to warm up. I run a little more hot water into the tub to slowly lift her body temperature a bit more, and she squeezes her knees tighter to her chest, as though distinctly aware of how naked she is in front of me right now.

Finally, when she's able to talk again, she looks up at me, an apologetic expression on her face.

"I'm sorry," she mumbles. I can tell from the look on her face she's really annoyed with the way this went down, but sometimes, we have to make the mistake to find out we were screwing up.

"It's okay," I reply. Some part of me wants to chew her out for putting herself in such danger, but I know it wouldn't do any good. She's already having a hard enough time as it is, she doesn't need me scolding her on top of it.

"I just...I thought I could go out and come back quickly, I didn't think anything would happen," she continues, shaking her head, sending a small spray of water from the tips of her hair. "If you hadn't come out there looking for me, I don't even know what would have happened..."

"I did, though," I point out to her, gently. "So you've got nothing to worry about. You're safe. That's all that matters."

She lifts her gaze to look at me, and she manages a small smile.

"Thank you," she murmurs. "I – thank you, Nathan."

I nod.

"It's fine," I promise. "Come on, let's get you into bed so you can get some sleep – you're probably exhausted."

She nods, and I reach for a towel just before she stands up and reveals herself to me. She's not entirely in her right mind yet, and I know she would be mortified if she found out she had shown her naked body to me.

I wrap the towel around her, and I can't help but notice how small she feels in my arms – how soft, how delicate, like she might break at any moment. I feel a swell of protectiveness for her, and I know I have to ignore it. She doesn't need someone like me coming along, trying to tell her how to live her life, trying to act like I have the right. She made a silly mistake, and I was there to fix it. It doesn't go any further than that.

I lead her through to my bedroom, where I can keep an eye on her – I switch on the radiator next to the bed as she sinks into it, and I tug the covers up and over her. Her eyes are already starting to fall shut, the sleepiness getting the better of her.

I will keep an eye on her. I know tiredness can be a sign of worse things to come, and I'm not going to let anything happen to her. I'm sure I'm just being over-cautious, but I'd rather that than to let her get really ill from being out in the cold like that.

I sit on the edge of the bed and watch as her breathing smooths out, starting to settle down into a regular pace. The color has returned to her cheeks, and she looks a whole lot better than she did. She turns to face me in her sleep, and her lips part slightly, as though she is on the brink of saying something.

I reach out to brush a strand of her wet hair back from her face, my fingers brushing against her cheek for the barest moment. And, as she sleeps, her lips curl up briefly into a smile.

Chapter Seven – Emmy

When I wake up, it's to find myself in a different bed than the one I expected.

I lift my head and look around, furrowing my brow as I try to remind myself just where I am – and that's when it hits me. I remember everything that happened out in the cold, falling into Nathan's arms, and having him carry me back to the cabin before he gave me a bath and took me to bed.

Not like *that*, of course, but still. I'm in his room right now, and I peer around, wondering if it's all really over that easily. I think I am okay, even though my body still aches from all the shaking and trembling I did before. My limbs feel like cement laying against the bed, and I groan as I sink back into the pillow.

I have no idea how long I have been here, but it's dark outside. Is Nathan mad at me? He must be. Having to run after me like that and bring me back from the brink when he had already told me I should know better than to go out into the snow must have been infuriating for him.

Not to mention having to help me get undressed and into a bath when I got back. I feel my cheeks burning at the thought – oh, my God, he saw everything. As in, every little part of me. I can hardly believe it. I might have thought he was hot, but there was no way I ever would have chosen to let him see me like that. Hardly the most seductive thing in the world is it...?

I peer beneath the covers and see that I'm naked, the towel I got out of the bath in tossed to one side. The bed is a little damp, but it's still perfectly warm, and I don't want to get out of it. I am sure he's about ready to get some sleep himself, after everything I put him through, but I don't know if I want to climb out of bed and go to my room to get dressed. He's probably already seen enough of me to last a lifetime, more than he ever intended to.

There is a slight knock at the door, and it opens opposite me. I pull the covers around my waist and sit up, trying to ignore the tension in my muscles as I move.

"Nathan?" I blurt out, as though it could be anyone else.

"Hey, Emmy," he replies. He's carrying a tray, with a bowl and a cup on it, both of them steaming with heat. I feel my stomach grumble hungrily and wonder how long I've been out.

"I'm so sorry," I tell him before he can say another word. I need him to know that this isn't how I wanted this to go down, I didn't expect to need his help like that. Normally, I'm not quite so stupid, but clearly my brain hasn't taken well to the cold.

"It's okay," he replies, as he plants down the tray on the bed beside me. " brought you some soup and tea. You need to eat and get some fluids in you. You've been through a lot."

I reach for the cup and lift it to my lips, taking a long sip of the sweet, steaming liquid. I close my eyes and let out a sigh. I can't believe how much trouble I got myself into so quickly, I couldn't have been out of the cabin more than a half-hour, but I had already started to wilt.

"Thank you," I murmur to him. It seems the least I can say in the face of everything he has done for me, and I hope he knows how grateful I am right now. I know it must have been a pain in his ass to see me ignore the advice he gave me and then have to run after me the way he did.

"It's okay, I told you," he assures me. "You shouldn't have been out there, but I understand it. It's hard to know how serious things can get if you're not used to that kind of temperature. People don't expect it in a place like Tuscany, but it can get rough out here."

I nod.

"Yeah, I think I'm starting to get that now," I agree, with a sigh, and I silently vow not to do anything so stupid again in my life. I don't want to have to drag him out of the comfort of his cabin to save me again.

"You need to rest," He tells me. "You stay through here, it's warmer in my room than yours."

I nod, chew my lip. I don't know why, and I'm sure he's going to think I'm insane for even thinking it, but I want him to stay with me through the night. I don't know what it is, but being alone right now seems a little unsettling to me, and I have no idea how I'm going to get through this evening after the scare I had earlier in the day.

"Nathan?" I whisper, before I take another sip of my tea. Oh, hell, am I really going to say this to him? He'll think I'm insane, I'm sure of it.

"Yes, Emmy?"

"Will you...sleep in here with me tonight?" I ask him. I hold my breath as I wait for a response. He's going to say no, of course he is, not a chance in hell he'll go along with that. He stares at me for a moment, as though he's not sure he's heard me right.

"You want me to...?"

"I'm sorry, I shouldn't have brought it up," I blurt out. "I didn't mean anything but it. I'm just freaked because of what happened today, I don't want to be alone, that's all..."

He eyes me for a long moment, and then, slowly, he nods.

"No, I understand," he replies. "I can bring through another set of covers, we can sleep on opposite sides if you want. Would that help?"

I smile. He gets it. Thank goodness. I'm not sure I would have been able to make it through the evening without someone there to help me. He's already done so much, but I don't want this to be over, not quite yet, not when it feels so good to have him near me.

"Yeah, it would help," I reply, and he smiles.

"Okay, I'll bring the stuff through," he replies. "You finish up your food, okay? I'll see you in a little while."

"Thanks, Nathan," I tell him, and I mean it with every fiber of my being. I am so grateful for how he has treated me today, how well he has taken care of me, even though I am not sure I really deserve it.

I wish I could have gotten in contact with my mom, because I would have told her there is nothing for her to worry about – I'm with someone who knows how to take care of me.

And I know everything is going to be okay.

Later that evening, Nathan pulls through the covers and lays them out on the bed, so there's a little space between us, no chance of us actually touching during the night. I am still undressed beneath the covers, but it doesn't bother me like it did when I first woke up. I'm all warm and toasty in bed, and the thought of getting to steal a little of his body heat is comforting.

I know Lyla would lose her actual shit if she found out I was sleeping in the same bed as her dad. I am not even sure what I think I am doing here, why I need him next to me, but there is a part of me I can't deny that does – a part of me that wants him close, even though I know it's wrong, even though I know it's crazy.

He strips to the waist and slides into the bed beside me, and I hold my breath as he shifts into position. Being in his arms earlier, even as out of it as I was, I couldn't help but notice how strong he is, how powerful. Those workouts seem to have done him a whole lot of good.

"Are you okay?" He murmurs to me softly, his voice as gentle as the low light of the snow through the window above me. I nod.

"I'm good," I promise. I close my eyes, and, listening to the slow sound of his breathing, I fall into a peaceful sleep.

When I wake the next morning, I feel something strange against me – something I haven't felt for a long time before. It takes me a moment to work out just what it is, but when I do, my mind jolts me awake.

It's his hand. Resting on my waist. Not gripping, not holding, not pulling me towards him, but just resting there. His thumb skims against my skin as he sleeps, his long, slow breaths reminding me he's still out for the count.

Oh my God. What happened? I thought we were keeping our distance while we were sleeping, but now...

I don't know how it happened, but the covers have been tossed aside, and we're under one comforter now. His body is just a few inches away from me, and I can feel his breath on the back of my neck. I know this is probably nothing more than an instinct for him, and there doesn't need to be anything read into it, but still...

The comfort of his hand on my waist is almost more than I can make sense of, and I don't want to pull away. Slowly, carefully, trying not to disturb him too much, I shuffle back towards him in bed. I'm still naked, and I feel utterly and completely exposed. And yet, not vulnerable at all. As though I am the one with all the power here.

As I move towards him, his hand slips to my hip, and I feel his fingers digging in to my skin lightly. A shock of arousal rushes through me. I don't know what is happening, but I don't want it to stop. In the cool morning light, this man has his hands on my naked body, and I need more. Badly.

I shift till I am pressed back up against him, my body nestled into the cradle of his. Underneath his sweatpants, I can feel something starting to stir, and I hold my breath. Is this really happening? I know I should stop this, know I should pull back before it goes any further, but I can't, I don't want to. This is my best friend's dad, and yet...

As I feel his hand slide to my lower belly as he pulls me against him, as I feel his lips graze over the back of my neck, nothing else in the world matters. I haven't felt want like this in such a long time, and knowing this man, this man who I am sure could have anyone in the world he wants, seems set on me, is more than I can take.

Is he awake? I swear, I can hear his breathing change, as though something has shifted within him. I want to turn my head and look at him, but I know, if I do, I might break the spell, and I'm not ready to do that yet. I don't know what to say, what to do, but I don't want this to stop. I don't want this moment to end.

His hand traces down, towards the apex of my thighs, and his fingers graze against my mound. We're doing this. We're really doing this. I push myself back against him, feeling the hardness of his cock beneath his pants, and I know I need to feel him inside me. I crave it, the burning need almost more than I can take.

"You want this?" He murmurs to me, his lips grazing against my ear as he kneads my mound softly. I nod.

"Yes," I breathe back, hardly able to get the words out. "Yes, I want this."

He pushes down his pants and I part my legs, hardly able to catch my breath. This is so wrong, but my body is still crying out for it in ways I can't deny. I don't want this to end. I don't want him to stop. And, as he brings his cock to my slit for the first time, I can't help but let out a groan of pleasure.

He slides his hand down another inch, massaging my clit as he eases himself inside of me. He takes his time, going slow, and thank God, because his cock is bigger than any other I've been with before. I groan as he slips into me, filling me with his full length, hardly able to keep my head straight as he penetrates me. He plants a kiss on the back of my neck as he toys with my clit expertly, and I feel myself give in to it, to the heavenly feeling of being with him in this way I know I shouldn't.

Once he is all the way inside of me, he begins to move – slowly at first, letting me get used to the feel of him, and then, he begins to pick up the pace. I reach back to grab his hip and pull him into me, listening to the sound of his breath starting to grow more ragged as he fucks me. I love knowing that I am turning him on, that he's hardly able to hold back as he takes me like this.

Outside, the snow is still falling, and it's as though we are in a little cocoon together, away from the real world, away from any of the implications that might come with doing something like this. Outside, people would judge us both, think we were crazy for even touching each other, but as he slides himself deep into me, all of that just seems to fall away. I can't think of anything but how much I want this, how much my body craves him, and I don't want anything to get in the way of it.

He wraps his arm around me and pulls me against him hard, driving himself even deeper into my pussy as he starts to pant against my neck. I want to turn around and kiss him, but the orgasm is teetering so close to the edge right now and I am determined to take it before this ends. I don't know what the hell we are going to do when he pulls out of me, when this is over, but I don't care. Right now, all I can think about is the feeling of his hard cock in my pussy, and how much I want it, I crave it, and need more of him!

He pinches my clit lightly between his fingers, and I let out a long moan as the orgasm finally courses through me, my pussy clenching around his cock. I feel as though our bodies are melding together, no space between us any longer, everything blurring until the only thing I can think of is him inside me, his mouth on my neck, his breath in my ear, all of it.

He holds himself deep inside of me, and a few moments later I feel him reach his own release – the warmth of his release as he finishes in me, the intimacy of it not lost on me. Slowly, slowly, as though he doesn't want this moment to be over, he pulls out of me – and I turn to face him.

He gazes at me for a moment, as though he is seeing me for the very first time, and I know just how he feels. After so long knowing each other through his daughter, here we are, in bed together, like we were always meant to be. It feels impossible, impossibly good, and I am not sure I can wrap my head around it.

So, I resolve not to. Why do I have to make sense of anything at all? This is just between us right now, and nobody else needs to know a thing about it.

I lean towards him, and plant a kiss on his lips, our first kiss, even as my body shudders from the orgasm he just gave me. He grins against my lips, and slides his hand into my hair to pull me closer and kiss me harder.

I have no idea what happens now. But, as he kisses me, it is hard to care about anything but how good it feels.

Chapter Eight – Nathan

I feel a pair of arms wrap around me as I make coffee at the kitchen counter, and I grin as she rests her head against my back.

"Good morning," she mumbles against me.

"Good morning," I reply, as I pour us both a cup coffee. "Coffee, emm?"

"I'd love one." she replies, as she pulls away from me and stretches, peering out of the window. "Is the storm still going?"

"Yeah, we're still stuck," I tell her, and she pulls a face and laughs.

"Oh, no," she jokes, as she takes the coffee from me. "I can't imagine how we're going to pass the time now. jokingly?"

I can't help but lean forward and give her a kiss. I'm sure this is crazy, but I'm even more sure that it feels too right to put a stop to it now. I slide an arm around her waist and pull her in close, and she nestles against me happily, as though this is the only place in the world she wants to be.

I am doing my best not to think about what is going to happen when this storm is over, because I'm sure it's going to be a whole mess. But right now, right here, it's just the two of us, and I can't think of anything more important or more inviting than being with her, staying with her.

It's been a few days since our first hook-up, in my bed, and we've been sharing it ever since. Waking up next to her, it's a novelty I'm not sure I'm going to get tired of. There's something peaceful about being next to her, looking over and seeing the soft rise and fall of her chest and the slowness of her breathing. Her hair splayed out on the pillow around her, lit by the morning rays of the sun, as though she stepped right out of a painting.

It's the first time I've really let myself near anyone since the divorce, and the sense of freedom is palpable. After having my ego stamped on the way Natalie did, there's something so delicious about enjoying her company, knowing she really wants me. She doesn't know much about my marriage or what led to the end of it, but I don't need her to. All I really care about now is having her all to myself, and letting myself get lost to the sweetness of being wanted again.

And by a woman as gorgeous as her, too. I know there's a big age gap between us, but as long as it doesn't bother her, I'm not going to let it bother me. There's something so hot about knowing she desires me, knowing this woman who could have basically any man she wanted at a snap of her fingers is focused on me, of all people.

I'm sure my daughter would be furious if she knew what was going on, but it's not like she'll ever have to know. I'm sure Emmy's in no rush to tell her about it, either. I mean, this is probably something she'll look back on as a filthy little fling, the kind of taboo-breaking she just felt like she had to do, because she was young, because she was free, because she could. I hoped she wouldn't see me as some kind of pervert, taking advantage of her.

Judging by how much she seems to be enjoying the sex, I think I'm safe from that analysis. I love hearing the sounds she makes when she cums, the way her whole body tenses as though she is on the edge and doesn't want to hold back. She's so expressive in how much she wants me, and it's been a long time since I could truly say that and mean it. She can't get enough of me, touching me every chance she gets, running her hands over my body, admiring me. It's addictive, being wanted that much, and I don't know how I am going to step away from it when we're out of this cabin.

Because there's just no way we can make this work in the real world, is there? Surely not. I'm certain she'll want to end it the moment we set foot back on solid ground again. I'm trying not to think about that part. Live in the moment, right? And I'm doing my very best to be here, with her, right now.

I get the fire started, and the two of us sip on our coffee as the snow continues to fall outside. Normally, I would be getting a little cabin fever, being stuck in here so long, but with her, it doesn't seem to hit me as hard. How can it? I just want to lock those doors and pretend there isn't so much as a world outside, so we can just be together and forget about everything and everyone else.

She tangles her legs with mine on the couch as she gazes into the fire, leaning her head on my shoulder. It's this casual touch that drives me crazy, as though she just wants to be close to me. Before the divorce, Natalie and I had been drifting apart for a long time, and it's been hard for me to accept that my body is enough for someone. But Emmy? It seems enough for her.

I drape an arm around her shoulders, and she snuggles in to me as she takes a sip of her coffee, which I've made just the way she likes it.

"You know, I don't even think you can legally call that coffee any more," I remark to her. "There's so much sugar in it..."

"It still counts!" She replies, laughing. "If it gives me a hit of caffeine, then I think it still falls under the coffee umbrella, doesn't it?"

"You'd have to take it up with the coffee people," I remark.

"You must know some coffee people," she replies. "Guys like you have people for everything, don't they? You must have someone to pick out your coffee for you."

"Guys like me?" I ask her, cocking an eyebrow.

"Yeah, you know, guys with money," I explain. "You have people to get your cars, your houses...why not your coffee too?"

"I think I've been missing out," I reply. "I need to get someone to buy my coffee for me. You've got me feeling like I've been doing it all wrong."

She laughs, and shifts a little closer to me. I like hearing her laugh. There's something about it that's so comforting, knowing I don't have to push myself to be someone I'm not when I'm around her.

We chat a little more, about nothing in particular – both of us trying to avoid the topic of what is going to happen when we leave this cabin. I'm sure there's so much I want to ask, but I have no clue where to begin.

As she finishes up her coffee, I see the little glint in her eyes, the glint that I am starting to recognize. She trails her finger over my arm, up to my neck, and brushes it over my lip – I don't know what it is, but something about her casual touch turns me on more than anything.

"You know, I think it's only fair I thank you for the coffee," she tells me, her voice dropping, as she moves her hand down towards my crotch. My cock is already starting to rise at her words, and she knows it. She knows she has me just where she wants me, that I need her more than I can make sense of.

"If you insist," I murmur back, and she plants her lips against mine as she unzips my pants slowly, working her hand into my underwear to wrap her fingers around my erection.

Her touch is almost unbearably hot to me, and I can't help but moan against her lips as I feel her caress on me. She slips her tongue into my mouth, her hand sliding around the back of my neck to pull me in closer, and I reach over to grope at her thighs, feeling her soft curves beneath my hand. I don't know what it is about her, but when we're this close, it's as though everything else just falls out of my mind. Nothing matters.

Nothing but her.

She kisses me deeply as she begins to stroke my cock, taking her time, teasing me until I think I will hardly be able to take any more – and then, she slips down between my legs, kneeling on the floor in front of me and gazing up at me. My cock is just an inch or two from her mouth, so close I can actually feel her warm breath against my skin, but it's still not enough. I want more. I want her.

She plants a long, slow kiss on my tip, slowly swirling her tongue around the head before she takes a couple of inches into her mouth. I groan and let my head sink back on the couch behind me. Her lips feel velvety-smooth around me, and the softness as she slowly guides me into her mouth is almost painfully good. I steal a glance down at her, and the sight of her with my erection between her lips burns itself on to my brain at once.

She moves down as far as she can go, and then meets her lips with her hand to create a seal over my whole hard-on. She takes her time as she begins to slide up and down, massaging my length with her hand and her lips and her tongue, the pleasure rolling out to consume my whole body. I feel her let out a moan against me, the vibrations shuddering all the way up my torso, and I love knowing she is enjoying this as much as I am. She seems to savor having me like this, getting to pleasure me, and I am sure as hell not going to argue with it.

She begins to pick up the pace, using her saliva as lubricant to let her hand move more smoothly. I spread my arms over the back of the couch, and watch her. There is something so impossibly hot about the sight of her going down on me, the sight of her with my cock in her mouth, as though she can't get enough. She locks eyes with me, and I see a flash of devilish playfulness there, a sure sign she is getting off on this as much as I am.

She moans around me as she continues, taking as much of me into her mouth as she can, and it doesn't take long till I can feel myself drawing closer to the edge. I am going to cum soon, and she doesn't move her mouth, sliding up and down my length like she can't get enough.

She plants one hand on my thigh, and I can feel the vibrations of her moans shuddering down the full length of my cock. She knows just what she's doing, and the thrill of it, of having all her attention trained on me, is everything I need right now. I push up into her mouth, pressing myself deeper into her, and, a moment later, I find my release.

I let out a long, deep groan of pleasure as the orgasm finally takes control of me, my body tensing against her as she swallows down my seed. She doesn't move her mouth, eyes closed like she's savoring every drop, until I am done, when she slowly pulls back and flicks her tongue over her lips. She grins at me, a little cocky, but it's hard to care when she's just made me come that hard.

"Fuck," I murmur, and I pull her up beside me, burying my face into her neck. I inhale the scent of her, losing myself to the deliciousness of it. And, as I hold her close, I try not to think about how close this is to being over.

Chapter Nine– Emmy

When I wake up beside him, I can't help but smile.

I know I should know better than to let myself enjoy this as much as I am, but how can I not? How can I deny myself? The way he looks, just lying there beside me, his face soft as he sleeps, is impossibly lovely. I want to stay in this moment forever.

I reach out to trace my fingers over his jaw and lips. He looks younger when he's asleep, face relaxed, not carrying any of the tension it normally does, and I wonder what he's dreaming about.

Me? Maybe. I know I dreamt of him last night, dreamt of being at dinner with him back in New York. And yes, I know it's an impossible fantasy, but it's hard not to let my mind stray there, no matter how stupid I know it is.

Because this storm is going to clear soon, and I am certain I need to focus on what is going to happen when it does. We can't keep doing this. If Lyla finds out, she'll kill me – or him, or both, depending on how she feels. What I'm doing is a betrayal to her, I know that, but it's hard to care when it feels so good.

And anyone outside of this would look at our relationship and think I was a gold-digger, and he was just some creepy older guy buying a younger woman with his billions. I know how people think, and I know there's no way they would let a couple like us get away with being together.

Which is fine, because I'm sure he doesn't want a thing to do with me outside of this, not really. This is a guy who could have the hottest, coolest, richest, smartest women on the planet hanging off his every word, and I'm sure he's not into some college graduate who's barely in her mid-twenties.

And what, would we just stay together after this? Did I want that? To be with a man so much older than me? I have no idea. I've never really considered the possibility of being with an older guy, but honestly, there's something to be said for it. He has a maturity to him, a confidence I really like. I've been with a few guys over the years, but none of them have made me feel the way he does...

Before my mind can stray any further, his eyes open slowly, and he catches me looking at him. He reaches over to pull me against him, and I snuggle against his body happily.

"Good morning," he murmurs against my hair, and I nuzzle into his neck.

"Morning," I purr back. "You sleep well?"

"Actually, yeah," he replies, stretching and flipping over to face me. "It's been a while since I've slept so well. Must be the mountain air."

"I don't get any credit for tiring you out?" I shoot back playfully, and he laughs.

"Yeah, I guess you deserve some of the credit," he agrees, and he lays his head on the pillow and just gazes at me for a second. I gaze back. For a moment, it's hard to remember who he is, that he's the father of my best friend, that, up until a week or so ago, I was totally intimidated by him. Because, here, now, it feels as though the two of us were meant to find each other like this, and I don't want anything to change it.

We roll out of bed and make breakfast, getting on with our day. There is something domestic and sweet about spending time with him like this, though I am sure I should try to deny it. I need to hold myself back, keep myself from falling too much for this simple, quiet way of life. It's way too easy for me to get comfortable with it, and I'm sure I should know better.

As we sit to have our coffee and watch the snow falling peacefully outside, I notice a small dent in his ring finger. I knew he was married up until recently, but the two of us haven't really talked about it.

"Can I ask you something?" I wonder aloud, and he turns to me and nods.

"Of course, you can."

I take a deep breath.

"Why did you split up from your wife?"

He pauses for a moment, clearly not sure how to answer that question. I want to take it back at once, cursing myself for thinking it was appropriate.

"I'm sorry, you don't have to answer that," I blurt out, but he shakes his head.

"No, it's fine," he promises me. He pauses for a moment, looks to the window, gathering his thoughts.

"She...she met someone else," he explains. "I think we were really only staying together for Lyla. We hadn't felt the romance there for a long time, not really, and things just...came to an end."

He shakes his head, and runs his finger over the spot where his ring must have been once. I reach for his hand.

"It must have been so hard," I reply, and he gives me a slightly sad smile.

"In some ways, yes," he agrees. "But in others...well, in others, I wouldn't have been able to do this with you. And this is the most damn fun I've had in years."

I grin back at him. Now, that's what I like to hear. There's something about the way he looks at me when he says that that makes my hair stand on end, the back of my neck prickling with excitement. When he looks at me, makes me the focus of his attention like this, I feel like I am the most important thing in his life.

Even though I know it can't last.

I look to the window, where the snow is beginning to thin slightly.

"It's going to clear out there soon," I remark, shaking my head. "We can go back to civilization."

"I guess so," he agrees, and the two of us pause, sitting there in silence. Neither of us want to bring it up, to ask the question of what is going to happen when all of this is over, but I know I want to. I'm having so much fun with him, our connection intense, and the thought of throwing it all away when this is over is almost more than I can take.

I steal a glance at him out of the corner of my eye, trying to read his face for some hint of the way he feels about all of this, but I can't make one out. He doesn't want to let me know, and I don't understand him well enough to be able to tell what is going through his head in that moment.

We finish our coffee, and curl up on the couch together to watch a movie – something old, a black-and-white classic thriller that I can hardly pay attention to because his arm is draped along my shoulders casually. His gentle touch always makes my head spin in the best way possible, and I can't think straight with his thumb gently caressing my upper arm.

He is so caring, so delicate with me, as though he sees me as some eminently breakable thing he doesn't want to cause any harm to. It's the same way I felt when he brought me in from the cold, making sure I was okay, taking care of me so gently and so carefully as though I am precious to him.

"But am I?" I don't know. And the confusion is starting to drive me a little crazy. I wish I had the nerve to come out and ask, but I am worried I will shatter this moment, bring it all crashing down around me. This is so good, so special, and the thought of losing it is enough to make me burn with fear.

I doze off on his shoulder, dreaming again of the two of us back in New York – his hand on my waist as he steers me through a crowd, his voice in my ear as he makes sure I am okay. Just gentle, easy touches, a promise he is not going anywhere, a promise this means something to him as much as it means something to me.

And when I wake, he is brushing his fingers through my hair, helping me doze. I feel my heart swell with the tenderness of it. Lifting my head, I smile at him.

"You want to share some wine?" I suggest. He nods.

"You go pour us a glass of wine, I'll get the fire going," he replies, and he drops a kiss on my cheek before I rise to my feet and head to the kitchen.

I pour us both a glass of wine, and come back to find he has stoked the fire to a crackling blaze; it's so cozy, it almost feels illegal. I hand him his glass of wine, smiling.

"Thank you," he replies, and he draws me in for a kiss – his lips graze mine, and everything seems to slow to a halt for a moment. My heart stutters in my chest, and I wonder if it is possible I will ever feel this way again.

He smiles, brushes his nose against mine before he pulls back.

"What was that for?" I breathe, smiling right back at him.

"You just looked so damn tempting," he murmurs, and he kisses me again. And, as he draws me against him hungrily, I know he is far from done with me. Far from done with this.

And that our night is only just beginning.

Chapter Ten – Nathan

She rests her head on my lap, her breath coming slowly and steadily as she sleeps below me. I gently play with her hair, listening to the steadiness of her breathing, and sipping on what's left of the wine.

The fire has started to burn down to embers, glowing bright red, in front of us, but I am not quite ready to call it a night yet. I know I should soon, but this closeness I get to enjoy with her is just a little too much for to end so quickly.

She's mostly naked underneath the blanket she wrapped around herself when we were finished fucking and her soft, flawless skin splayed out below me. I trace down just behind her ear, caressing the spot when her throat meets her neck, and she shivers and smiles in her sleep.

I love watching her like this. When she is sleeping, and it's just the two of us, I can pretend there is no end in sight for us.

The snow is starting to clear outside, but neither of us really want to talk about what is going to happen when all of this is over. When we have to be honest with one another about what is going on, what we have, and what we're going to need to end soon.

Because there is no way she'll want to be with someone like me back in the real world. She's young, she doesn't want to be with someone with a daughter and a divorce under his belt – I mean, she was asking me about the divorce earlier in the day. She can hardly wrap her head around something like that, the enormity of it, and she shouldn't have to, not when she's so young.

Not to mention Lyla. I can't even imagine how my daughter would react if she found out I had gotten involved with one of her friends. She would freak out, no doubt about it, and with good reason, too. I mean, what kind of creep would I have to be to make that kind of move on one of her friends? Sleeping together is one thing, but turning it into something more serious...yeah, it's not something I can imagine.

And I doubt she can, either. Maybe there's a part of her, like there's a part of me, that wants to believe this can work. But the intensity of being alone together like this isn't going to survive when the two of us leave this cabin. How could it?

This is a fun fantasy to live in, but I know how people would look at me if I was to go through a divorce and then turn up with a younger woman on my arm. No matter what the reality, it would change the way people looked at me. They'd think I was just waiting to drop my wife to get with a girl twenty years younger than me, but it's nothing like that.

I could never have imagined that I would feel the way I did about someone like Emmy. Her sharpness, her wit, her curiosity about the world around her – all of it fascinates me, and I can't deny how much fun it is to be with her sexually, too. The chemistry between us feels impossible sometimes. I don't know if I've ever felt this before, not for anyone, and there's something about it I can't run from. Something about it I can't deny…

She shifts on my lap, and I trace my fingers over her cheek softly. God, she is so beautiful, just looking at her feels like I am breaking the rules somehow. I suppose I must have noticed it before, but I've done my best to pretend I don't see how strikingly gorgeous my daughter's best friend is.

I still don't know what Lyla will do when she finds out, though I have a good idea. She's never taken too well to the divorce, let alone her mother moving on. What would she do if she found out about this? About us…?

I sigh and stare into the dying embers of the fire. I know I need to leave this behind. I need to accept this is just a little fling, to get my dating feet back under me again, a way for me to ensure my passion is there the way it's always been. After feeling as though it was snatched from me by my ex, I know now I still have it in me, the way I did before.

I carefully lay her down on the couch and go to put out the fire, the sleepiness getting the better of me. I scoop her up into my arms and she snuggles against me, smiling in her sleep, as I carry her towards my bed. Our bed, now, I suppose, since we've been sharing it for the last week or so.

It's hard to believe it has only been a week, when this seems like it could go on forever. So removed from the rest of the world I can't help but wonder what it would be like if I could just find a way to let this keep going somehow. I know it's crazy, stupid for me to even think about it, but I can't help but entertain the idea.

I lay her down in bed, and undress, pulling the covers over the two of us as she reaches for me sleepily. She sighs as she nestles into my chest, her face pressed against my skin, as though there's nowhere else in the world she would rather be.

I kiss the top of her head, and close my eyes. With her here, I can actually sleep, instead of tossing and turning, running through the questions about my ex and my divorce and what happened there. I feel like she has given me the tools to move on at last, and I am beyond grateful for that.

I let myself doze off. No need to overthink this, no anymore. Right now, all that matters is that she is wrapped up here in my arms, and the rest of the world can wait a while before it gets anywhere close to us.

Chapter Eleven – Emmy

I toy with my coffee as I watch him, my eyes tracing out the shape of him right there in front of me. Does he know how handsome he looks right now?

I have no idea. I almost want to bring it up, but something tells me to keep my mouth shut. I have no idea how he would react, and I know the two of us are inching dangerously close to something more serious. As much as I try to push my feelings for him down, the comfort of being close to him is impossible to deny, and I can't bear the thought of this coming to an end soon.

He glances over his shoulder, as though able to feel my eyes on him.

"You okay?" He asks, and I nod quickly.

"Yeah, yeah, I'm fine," I assured him. I'm certain he is already looking forward to getting out of here, though he is too polite to say anything about it. I almost want to ask, what he's going to do when he leaves, what plans he has when this is over, but acknowledging it seems impossible right now.

I can't believe I've let this happen. I've let myself fall for him. I know I should have stopped myself a long time ago, I should have put some emotional barriers in place before I drew in too close, but it's too late for that now. When I look at him, I feel a warmth blooming through my chest, something deep and loving and wanting, and I can't just uproot it out of nowhere.

The snow is beginning to clear outside, and I'm sure we only have a few more days at most before this is over. Do I tell him what has been going through my mind? It seems dangerous, but maybe even more so to keep it to myself.

This was meant to be a chance for me to blow off some steam, leave behind the stress of college, but instead, I have just managed to dump a whole new stressor onto my mind. I can't believe I've been so stupid as to let my feelings get the better of me. I really thought I was stronger than that, but I can see I am nothing more than this hopeless romantic, falling for a man I know I can never have.

He joins me at the table, and a smile crosses over his face. I love his smile; there's something so warm and genuine about it, as though he wants to make sure I believe it.

"It's starting to warm up out there," he remarks. "The snow's beginning to clear. I think tomorrow we could try and get back down to the airport, if you like."

I chew on my lip and nod. I know he's right. I'm sure his company needs him back, sooner rather than later, and I don't want to keep him from it. But...but I am not sure if I can be done with this so easily. No without telling him what is on my mind, anyway.

"What are you going to do when you get back out there?" He asks with interest. "Start looking for a job, I guess?"

"Yeah, I guess," I echo. I can hardly think about what I am going to do when I leave this cabin, honestly. It feels like everything is revolving around this place, and walking out will bring the world crashing down around me. I don't like the thought of it.

"Something on your mind?" He asks me. He sounds concerned. Oh, I wish he didn't care as much as he did. It might have been easier for me to lie if I could just brush him off, if I could just act like he didn't give a damn about me, but I wasn't going to get so lucky. When it came to him, when it came to us, he seemed to be able to see a part of me I didn't want to show anyone else, and it would have been dangerous to hide it.

I take a deep breath, and look up at him. I know I need to do this, I need to see this through. I need to tell him what is bothering me so much, even if it is crazy and even if I know he is going to shoot me down. There might be a chance he feels the same way, and I know I won't be able to get over it unless I try to come clean with him and be honest about what is going on.

"Nathan, there's something I need to tell you," I confess, finally, haltingly, managing to get the words out of my mouth. He lifts an eyebrow at me, clearly confused.

"Okay?" He replies, and he reaches for his coffee. I reach out to take his hands, squeezing on them tightly, hanging on for dear life as though they are the only things keeping me pinned to Earth. If I let go of him, I am worried I will fall off the face of the planet, and not be able to find a way back.

"I...I know this is going to be over soon," I confess to him, forcing myself to keep talking, even though every part of me is screaming to just forget it. Just forget it, enjoy the last few days, then move on.

"And I know you have a whole life to get back to out there," I continue. "But there's something I need to tell you. And I'm aware of how crazy this sounds, so you don't need to tell me, I promise. I just...I need you to hear it, before we leave, so I can get it off my chest, alright?"

He nods, not saying a word. I can't read his expression. Does he know what I am about to say to him? I wish I could ask him to go first, to tell me how he feels about me, but I know there isn't a chance in hell I am going to be able to get him to come out with it. He's a private guy, keeps himself to himself unless he's pushed, and the best I can hope for is to tell him the truth and pray it's enough to get him to give me what I need in return.

I close my eyes. I can't even look at him as I say this. I just need to talk.

"I think I'm starting to fall for you," I confess to him. "No, I don't think it – I know I am. And I am so aware of how crazy it sounds, because both of us have lives to get back to outside this place, and they're so different – I know how hard it would be for us to be together, trust me, I've thought about all of it. I've thought about how much Lyla would hate the two of us for this, I've thought about how it would look, how everyone would see us if we were to come out as a couple. I've considered every single angle, and yet..."

I catch my breath, open my eyes, and look at him once more.

"And yet, it's not enough to convince me that I shouldn't do this," I tell him. "I'm really falling for you, Nathan. What we have here, it feels special, and I don't want it to be over just like that."

He stares back at me in silence, and I hold my breath, no idea what I want to say next. I don't know how to get this through to him, to convince him I really mean this. I just have to trust he understands I wouldn't say all of this as a twisted form of joke. I mean it. Every word I have said, I mean it, and now, he knows it, too.

"Do you understand me?" I ask him, my voice tiny. I hadn't realized how scared I would be until that moment, but sitting there, having just opened myself up in front of him, more or less splayed myself out before him, it feels like I am about to be ripped apart. I know we can't do this, I know he can't be with me, and yet, I find myself hoping, beyond anything, beyond everything, he will find a way to do this.

"Yes, I do," he replies, his eyes locked on to mine. I can't read his expression at all, and it scares me. Normally, I am able to tell what is going on inside his head, at least take a guess, but right now, I have nothing. I don't know what to say to him. I have come out with everything I needed him to know, and the ball is in his court now.

"And?" I prompt him. My heart feels like it is going to beat right out of my chest, but I still need to know what he's going to say. Even if it's just to turn me down, I have to hear it, it's the only way I am going to be able to move on...

"And" he begins, but before he can say another word, someone pounds on the door.

Both of us jump in surprise. Who the hell is that? We've been up here alone for nearly three weeks now, and nobody has come looking for us. He rises to his feet and makes his way to the door.

He pulls it open, and a man greets us both brightly. He is dressed in a heavy coat, thick boots, and gloves that look as though they could keep out an arctic wind chill.

"Ah, you're here!" He exclaims, as though surprised by the sight of us. "We thought some people were staying in this cabin – the car's been there a while, I came by to check if you needed any help getting out."

"Uh, yes, I think we do," Nathan replies, not looking back at me. I feel a pang in my chest. Oh. Okay. So he is done with this, then? He wants it to be over? He couldn't be making it much more obvious, and I suppose I shouldn't be surprised with the way he is acting right now. He didn't come into this looking for a long-term romance. Neither did I, for that matter, but I'm the one who let my feelings get the better of me.

"The roads are cleared now, I'm visiting all the cabins to make sure everyone knows," The man explains. "I'm the caretaker around here, we've probably met before. Nathan, is it?"

"Yes, that's right," Nathan replies. He sounds a little shell-shocked, and I am not sure if it has to do more with the man who has just turned up or with the confession I just dropped on his shoulders.

"I have a truck out there, I'd be happy to give your car a tow to get it back on the road," he suggests. He looks past Nathan, towards me, and I avert my eyes from him quickly. I am sure he will judge us, even though he has no right to. I don't want to deal with what he must be thinking about me, or Nathan, being up here all alone together.

"That would be great," Nathan replies. "Just give us a little while to gather our things, okay?"

"No problem," The man replies. "Mind if I come in? It's still freezing out there..."

Nathan waves him inside, and glances over at me. I know what he must be thinking. He just wants to get out of here. And he's telling me, in all the ways he can, to gather my stuff together and start to get ready to leave. We have a real world to get back to, and he doesn't want to wait any longer to return to it.

I rise to my feet, and trudge towards my room. I've hardly spent any time in there, given that I've been sleeping in his bed most nights, and it feels strange to be in there alone. I don't know what he thinks about what I told him, but he has made his desires pretty clear. He wants to get out of here. He wants to leave.

He wants this to be over.

And I don't have it in me to fight him.

Chapter Twelve – Nathan

I stare at the computer in front of me, trying to pull myself back together.

It's been nearly ten days since I got back from the cabin in Tuscany, and I know I should be doing a little better by now. I shouldn't be thinking about her anymore. She shouldn't have a claim to any space inside my head. And yet, she does.

I sigh, push my chair away from my desk, and turn to look out of the enormous glass window of my office and on to the city below.

It's so different to the cabin, the soft snow that surrounded us and insulated us from the rest of the world. I miss it, which feels crazy to say. I thought, when we first got stuck, I would be sprinting out of there when the time came, but now, all I wanted...

All I want is to go back.

We spent the car ride back to the airport together in silence. I had no idea what to say to her. Not after what she had confessed to me, not after the way things had changed. The last thing I had been expecting from her was to find out she had real feelings for me, and I wished I could find some way to convince her she didn't really want something long-term.

She might have believed she did, for now, at least but that was different than the reality of what it would have been like, the two of us together in the real world. Yes, it's fun for us to have our little fling while we're in the mountains together, but that's very different to actually dating.

Still…I can remember the way she looked at me, the way she gazed at me as she waited for a response, while I sat there, stupidly, utterly silent. And I wished I could tell her I wanted her, too. I wished I could tell her I needed her in the same way she needed me, that I had felt my feelings growing just the way she was describing.

It's stuck in my head, rotating around and around as I try to work out what to do about it. How can I make it right? I know I hurt her, I know I stung her, not giving her the response she wanted, but it's up to me to be the sensible one. It's up to me to be the one who can see the truth, even if it hurts. That we can't be together, because it would cause too many problems for both of us.

At least, that's what I have to keep telling myself. Because if I don't, if I stop, if I am really honest with myself about what I want, I crave her just as badly as I did the first time we were together.

I know she's back in New York now, same as me, and the two of us are going about our normal lives again. I haven't heard from her since, and I don't know if I have even crossed her mind again. I wouldn't be surprised if she has already moved on, got over her little mountain madness moment and moved on with her life. I wish I could just find a way to get back to her again, one more night, to get her out of my system, but even that I know would be a lie. It's the addiction to her I can't shake, the want to see her just one more time, but it would just make it worse.

I need to cut myself off entirely. It's the only way I can be safe, and I can keep her safe from whatever we have, too. Just because we have feelings for one another doesn't mean that we need to act on them. It doesn't mean that we are right for each other. Sometimes, people have chemistry, and it doesn't need to mean anything. It's just a quirk of fate, nothing more to it than that.

My secretary knocks on the door, and I lift my head, trying to calm my racing thoughts. I am meant to be running a billion-dollar company here, and I don't know how I'm going to stay on top of it with my mind on such a mess of emotion.

I lift my head and offer her a smile, hoping that she doesn't see what's going on behind my eyes right now. The last thing I want is to give anything away, and I'm sure I have come close enough to that as it is.

"You have a meeting in half an hour," she tells me. "Do you need me to organize your notes?"

"That would be great, thank you, Tabitha," I tell her, trying to keep my voice steady. I can't help but wonder what she would think of me if she knew about the fling I'd had with a woman as young as Emmy. She would probably imagine I was nothing more than some old pervert, trying to reclaim his glory days by seducing a woman twenty years younger than him, a way to get over his divorce or something.

She ducks out of the room, and I sigh. Why am I so worried about what people would think about me? People told me I didn't have a chance of getting this business off the ground, and I did. They told me I wouldn't be able to balance my work and having a family, but I had managed it. Why now, of all times, am I suddenly wringing my hands about what they will say about me, what they will think? It feels crazy, but at the same time, the thought of pushing away those worries scares me.

It will change everything in my life. Everything. If I admit how I feel about her, nothing stays the same. My whole life as I know it will be thrown into flux, and I don't know if I can risk it – I don't know if I can risk dragging her into that change, either.

But if I don't, I know I will be stuck in this office, unable to think about anything but her, how

much I want her, how much I miss her. And I
don't know if I can handle that, either.

Chapter Thirteen – Emmy

I stare at the ceiling, wondering when the void in my chest is going to clear. It's been there for so long, I don't know what I can do to make it soften.

It's been nearly two weeks since I got back from the cabin, and I feel as though I have been in stasis ever since. He didn't say a word to me about what I told him – when I confessed my feelings, we were interrupted before he could get anything else out, and I don't know what I am supposed to do to make it right.

No. Nothing. I don't have to do anything. He's clearly already made his mind up, and I am not going to be the girl stupid enough to go chasing him down when he's already decided what he wants. If he felt the same way, he would have said something to me by now, I'm sure of it, and I don't need to keep torturing myself by wondering what might have happened if he'd just had a chance to tell me what was on his mind.

We're done. Our little fling, it's over. And I just need to focus on getting back to my life and moving on, because this is starting to weigh too heavy on my shoulders.

Lyla is still in France right now, swooning all over her new man, and I don't want to interrupt her. I am not sure I could handle hearing about how amazing he is anyway – I'm having a hard enough time as it is, without her reminding me of just how much I am missing out on. Besides, not like I am going to talk to her about what happened in the cabin, about how it's her dad I am feeling all torn up over. She would lose it. I'm sure of it.

I have been putting in some new applications for work, but I have been half-hearted about all of them, if I was being honest. I want to move on, but how can I do that, when I never got a reply about how he really felt? It seems impossible, without some kind of closure, without some kind of sureness one way or another, and I don't know what I am supposed to do to get it.

He didn't even give me his number. I can't even call him to get to the bottom of this. I want to speak to him, to hear his voice again, but I have no right, and I'm sure I would just be interrupting his busy schedule if I tried to get in touch with him now. I was just a distraction for him, a way for him to get over his divorce. Nothing long-term. Nothing serious.

I can't help but feel used, even though that's on me. He didn't lead me on. He didn't promise anything he didn't see through. I just invented this fantasy in my head, and now, I'm burning with sadness it didn't come true.

My life outside college hasn't exactly started as I dreamed it would. I feel as though my heart is broken, shattered into pieces, and I can't believe I was foolish enough to think a man like him would ever really go for someone like me. Of course, he didn't. Of course he didn't want anything to do with me. He's smarter than that, older, more mature, and he doesn't want to be with someone right at the start of their adult life.

I pull myself off the couch with a dramatic sigh and trudge to the kitchen to make something to eat. Just a couple of weeks until Lyla is back, and I am sure she's going to be full of romance and wistfulness after what she experienced. I can't even talk to her about my own little love story, because it's with her… Dad!

I catch sight of myself in the window opposite the kitchen sink, and I can't help but notice how tired I look. I have been having a hard time sleeping while I've been away from him, and I don't know how long it's going to take for my schedule to get back to normal. The exhaustion, it's settling in to my system, the new normal, and I haven't even started my first real post-college job yet.

I need to meet someone new. Go out to a club, party, have fun, find a guy who makes my heart flutter…but even imagining it seems impossible right now. I try to picture myself with another guy, and all I can think about is being with Nathan. Feeling his hands on me, his tongue in my mouth, his body pushing against mine, his fullness inside me...

Ugh. No way can I cook when I'm this distracted. I'm going to order something in instead. I grab my phone and put in an order for some Chinese food. At least that's one of the plus sides about being back in the city, instead of out in a lonely cabin somewhere.

I flop back down on the couch to wait for it to arrive, and scroll through the contacts on my phone. I could reach out to Lyla, ask her for her dad's number, but I'm sure she would be on to me in a matter of seconds. I don't want her guessing what I have been up to.

A half-hour later, there is a knock on the door, and I drag myself to my feet to answer it. My stomach is grumbling, and I am starving, but the thought of having to actually speak to another human being doesn't really appeal right now.

I grab some money to pay the driver, and I pull open the door – and when I see who is standing on the other side, I freeze.

"Nathan?" I breathe, blinking, wondering if he is really there or if my cluttered brain is just inventing him because I want to see him so badly. I blink, waiting for him to vanish from existence in front of me, wondering what on Earth he is doing here.

But he doesn't move. He's not a mirage. He's really here. He's really standing there, just a few feet from me, so close I could reach out and touch him, the look on his face as unreadable as the last time I saw him.

"What are you doing here?" I blurt out, before I can stop myself. This doesn't seem fair. How can he just turn up? All this time thinking of him, wondering about him, dreaming of him, and now, he's standing in front of me as though it's the most natural thing in the world.

"I wanted to see you," he tells me, simply, as though it should be obvious. "Can I...can I come in?"

I nod. Step aside. Gesture for him to enter my little apartment. He steps inside, and it feels surreal, that he could be there right in front of me. After everything we've been through, everything that's happened, he's here, in my real life, as though it's where he belongs.

My heart is pounding in my chest, and it feels like it is going to burst right out. There is so much I want to say to him, so much I want to tell him, and I don't even know where to start. More than anything, I want to fall into his arms, wrap myself around him and pull him in close and beg him to stay, to just stay, even if it's hard, even if it's crazy.

He looks so out of place in my apartment. In his suit, his expensive suit, fresh from work, it looks as though he belongs more in a boardroom than my living room. But here he is, in front of me, and I am not going to pass up the chance to make the very most of it I can.

I swallow heavily. I don't even know where to start.

"Why are you here, Nathan?" I ask him, my voice catching at the back of my throat as I speak. But, before I can say another word, he turns around, and he kisses me.

My breath is knocked from my lungs as our lips connect again. I don't know what he is doing here, where this is going, but there is no way in hell I am about to argue with it, when it feels as good as this. I wrap my arms around him, and he lifts me off the ground, planting me on the edge of the kitchen counter and kissing me as hard as he can.

His hands are travelling all over my body, and I can't think about anything but how much I want him, how much I need this. I am sure I should know better than to just give in to this feeling, but I can't deny it – can't hide from it. I wrap my legs around him and pull him in close to me, feeling the pressure of his cock through his pants, needing him inside of me, needing to feel more.

He brushes his lips down to my neck, and I cradle his head in my hand, holding him as close as I can. Does he know how good he feels to me right now? Does he have any idea?

He pushes down my jeans and panties, and I grope for his erection, unzipping his pants and pulling it into my hand – he is already hard, as though he has been waiting for this for so long he just can't hold back any longer. I know how he feels. Panting against his mouth, I shift to the very edge of the counter so that we are just a few inches apart, my body tilted towards his, silently telling him everything he wants to hear.

"Please," I murmur to him, and he pushes apart my thighs with his knee, plants himself at my entrance, and slips all the way inside of me in one long thrust.

I gasp and sink against him, his fullness making my head spin. I reach down to the small of his back to push him deeper inside of me. Is this all a dream, a fantasy? I can't believe it's happening, but I don't want it to stop. Not when it feels this good, not when being near to him makes me feel this alive.

He drives himself into me, deep and hard, fucking me like it's the only thing on Earth he can think about. How long has he been holding himself back? All the time we have been apart? It's only been a couple of weeks but it feels like a lifetime, as though the two of us are coming together after being pulled away from each other for months.

I turn my head to kiss him, pushing my tongue into his mouth once more. I can't get enough of him. I don't know if I'll ever get the chance to do this again, if this is just one last fuck before we both move on, and I don't want to miss a moment of it. I want to lose myself to his taste, his touch, his caress, the way he feels, the way he makes me feel.

I can already feel the orgasm starting to grow inside of me as he thrusts deep into me, the warmth spreading out from my belly to consume every inch of my nervous system. He is panting into my ear, his breath ragged and tinged with want, and I love it – I love feeling him like this, love knowing I am enough to get him to this point of no return.

His body stiffens against mine, and he pushes in deep one last time – I feel him finish inside of me, his cock twitching, and he holds me close, his arms wrapped all the way around me like he doesn't want to let me go.

And it's that which takes me over the edge. I squeeze myself around him, the pleasure pulsing out from my pussy to cover my entire body. I can feel my nerves tingling, from my spine all the way to my toes and up to my scalp, and I can't think about anything else but how good it feels to be with him again.

He is still inside me when the doorbell buzzes – he pulls back, and I laugh at how he acts like he has been caught doing something he shouldn't have.

"It's just Chinese takeout," I assured him, as I shakily pull up my jeans and panties again. "Do you want to stay and share it with me?"

"Yeah, I would," He replies, running a hand through his hair and catching his breath. His cheeks are flushed, and I pause for a moment, just to look at him.

I am still not sure what he is doing here. But I am sure as hell not about to let him leave. Not until I work out what he wants from me.

And not until I get at least a little more of what I want from him.

Chapter Fourteen – Nathan

We sit at either end of her couch, the Chinese takeout between us, and I can't take my eyes off of her.

I can't believe I am really here. I got her address from Lyla, as casually as I could, saying she had left something behind I wanted to drop off. But in truth, it was just that I needed to see her. I need to give her a response to what she said to me back in the cabin, because I left it hanging, and I can't stand to think she might believe I don't feel the same way.

We finish up the Chinese takeout, and she bites her lip as she looks at me. Her eyes search mine, and I instantly feel bad that I've given her reason to doubt why I might be here. I don't want her to think this is just a hook-up to me, a chance to get my rocks off. This is more than that.

More than anything I have felt before in my life, actually.

"So," she begins, tucking a loose strand of hair behind her ear. "Am I allowed to ask what you're doing here now?"

I grin, nod. I got distracted when I laid eyes on her again, but now we're here, a little more clear-headed, I am glad for it. I know it's always going to be hard for me to keep my hands to myself when she's around, she's just too damn sexy for me to pretend otherwise.

"Yeah, I guess so," I reply. "I'm sorry to drop in on you like this out of the blue. I know I should have given you more warning. But honestly..."

I shake my head. I don't even know where to start. There is so much I want to say to her, so much I need her to know, and I haven't got a clue where I am supposed to begin.

"I haven't been able to stop thinking about you, not since we left the cabin," I confess to her. "I know we got interrupted before I could tell you how I felt, but if I'd had the chance, I would have told you...I would have told you that I feel the same way you do."

Her eyes widen. She catches her breath, holds it, as though making sure she doesn't disturb my words as they hang in the air before us.

"You do?" She asks, and she glances away from me. I am sure I can see tears flashing in her eyes, and I hate that I have made her doubt this for a moment. After all that happened, all that we went through, I need her to know I feel everything she does. No matter how hard it might be for her to believe.

"Yes, I do," I reply. "And I know how it sounds. I know how people are going to see us, I'm not stupid. But when I think about being with you, I just...I can't give a damn about it. I can't think about anything but how good it would feel to make this work, for real."

The corners of her lips quirk up into a smile – that gorgeous smile, that makes the hair on the back of my neck stand up. Everything else seems to fall away when she is smiling at me like that. I don't know how anything else in the world can matter, how anything else can even come close.

"You mean it?" She asks, and I nod.

"Yeah, I mean it," I promise. "I know it's not going to be easy. And I know it might not last forever. I know there's the age gap, I know we're at different points in our lives, I know Lyla might have something to say about it..."

She lets out a laugh.

"But I know I would never be able to forgive myself if I didn't do something to show you how I feel. Because...I want to be with you."

She pauses for a moment, closing her eyes, as though taking in what I have just said to her. I know it's big, bigger than anything we've done so far, but it's true.

"I haven't felt this way about anyone before in my life, Emmy," I continue. "And I thought, after the divorce, I never would. I didn't think it was truly possible. But when we were together..."

I trail off. I don't know how to put it into words, not exactly, but I know what I feel is real. I know I can't let go of what we had, and I don't want to miss out on the chance to try with her.

"No matter what people think, I want to see how this goes," I tell her. "If you'll give it a chance, too."

She nods, slowly. And I feel something shift inside of me, something powerful. Some part of me that wants her, wants this, more than anything in the world, is finally seeing the light. Not giving a damn what anyone else thinks or what they want. Because when I look at her, the world seems to dim, she is the only beam of light from a woman I've been looking for at this moment.

"I want to," She replies. "I want to try this, Nathan. And I know it's not going to be easy, I get that, but..."

She trails off, shakes her head.

"I think it's worth it, anyway," she finishes up. Her voice is small, but certain. It's all I need to hear.

I lean towards her, and plant a kiss on the corner of her lips. I can feel her smiling against me. I know what comes next isn't going to be easy, but as long as I have her, as long as we have each other, I can't find it in me to give a damn.

Epilogue – Emmy

"Hey!" I call to him, as I step into our apartment. He glances over from the kitchen, and lifts a ladle in greeting.

"Hey, babe," he calls back, and I grin. I love it when he calls me by my little pet name; it reminds me of how much he cares.

I head over to the kitchen, dropping my bag on the couch as I go, and give him a kiss. He grins against my lips.

"Good day at work?" He murmurs, and I nod.

"Yeah, I managed to get that artist I've been keeping an eye on to agree to an exhibition."

"Oh, wow!" He exclaims. "That deserves some wine..."

I watch as he goes to our wine rack and picks out the perfect bottle, and wonder just what I have done to deserve a man like this.

Hard to believe it's been nearly a year since we were locked up in that cabin together. And a crazy year, at that. Coming clean to our families about our relationship wasn't exactly easy, especially when it came to Lyla – but they came around. When they realized we really cared about each other, and it wasn't just some fling we'd put too much thought into.

"I get it," Lyla told me, one night, over a few glasses of wine, as the two of us had a heart-to-heart about it. "You fall for who you fall for. God knows it's happened to me..."

A few people from his work had judgments to cast, too, but he never let it get to him. The first time he came to an event with me on his arm, I could see people judging me, probably thinking I was just in it for the money, and it made me a little uncomfortable.

"I know you're here for the right reasons," he assured me, in the car on the way home afterwards. "You don't have to pay attention to what a single one of those assholes think."

I leaned my head on his shoulder; and grinned. He really saw me for who I was, not who everyone seemed to think I had become when we were together. I had to stay focused on that. Nothing else could matter.

It didn't take long for us to move in together. After spending all that time in the cabin together, it just made sense for us to be together full-time. We picked out a beautiful apartment on the Upper West Side, close to the gallery where I had just started work, and began to make a home together.

The apartment itself is covered in art, most of it pieces that I've picked out from the gallery; being with a billionaire has it's upsides, though I do my best to keep my feet on the ground wherever possible. There's no need for me to rely on him or his money to get ahead, when I have all the confidence in my own skills that I need.

He pops open the wine, and pours us both a glass; I take mine from him, and touch it against his.

"Congratulations," he murmurs to me, a warm smile on his face. "Seems like you're really excelling with your work lately."

"Hmm, would you expect anything less from me?" I reply, mostly joking. He laughs.

"I guess not," he agrees. "Is lasagna okay for dinner?"

"You know, you could just hire a chef," I remark to him. "Not like you haven't got the funds for it."

"And miss out on making you dinner?" He replies, raising his eyebrows. "Not a chance in hell. I like taking care of you."

"Well, I'm not going to argue with that," I agree. I take a sip of my wine and feel the warmth of it blossom through my chest as he goes back to making dinner. I am not sure I will ever get used to this, not really, the feel of knowing I have this sweet home to come back to.

But, with every day that passes, I am more and more grateful for it. More and more grateful we decided to give this a try.

And more and more certain it's going to last for
the rest of our lives.

The end.

Afterword

Dear Reader,

Thank you for joining me on this journey through "Fantasies of My Best Friends Dad: An Age-Gap Romance." It has been an honor to share this story with you.

As I wrote this novella, I found myself becoming deeply invested in the lives of the characters. I laughed with them, cried with them, and felt their passions, struggles, and triumphs as if they were my own. I hope that you, too, were able to connect with these characters and feel their emotions as you read.

This novella was not just a labor of love, but also a labor of growth. As an author, I pushed myself to explore new themes, experiment with different writing styles, and challenge myself in ways I never had before. I am proud of the result, and I hope that it has left an impact on you as well.

Whether you are a longtime fan of my work or a new reader, I'm grateful for your support. Your encouragement and feedback is invaluable to me as I continue this writing journey.

Thank you again for reading "Fantasies of My Best Friend's Dad: An Age-Gap Romance." I look forward to sharing more stories with you'll in the future. Check out my New release "My Billionaire Rancher: Secret Lover" ….

Warm regards,

Lavender Skye